ACKNOWLEDGMENTS

I thank God for bridges of words. Gracias a mi familia, mis amigos, Michelle Humphrey, Reka Simonsen, Sara Palacios, and the entire publishing team.

—M. E.

ATHENEUM BOOKS FOR YOUNG READERS
An imprint of Simon & Schuster Children's Publishing Division
1230 Avenue of the Americas, New York, New York 10020
Text © 2021 by Margarita Engle
Illustrations © 2021 by Sara Palacios
Book design by Karyn Lee © 2021 by Simon & Schuster, Inc.
All rights reserved, including the right of reproduction in whole or in part in any form.
ATHENEUM BOOKS FOR YOUNG READERS is a registered trademark of Simon & Schuster, Inc.
Atheneum logo is a trademark of Simon & Schuster, Inc.
For information about special discounts for bulk purchases, please contact Simon & Schuster Special Sales
at 1-866-506-1949 or business@simonandschuster.com.
The Simon & Schuster Speakers Bureau can bring authors to your live event. For more information or to book an event,
contact the Simon & Schuster Speakers Bureau at 1-866-248-3049 or visit our website at www.simonspeakers.com.
The text for this book was set in Century Expanded.
The illustrations for this book were digitally rendered.
Manufactured in China
0521 SCP
First Edition
2 4 6 8 10 9 7 5 3 1
Library of Congress Cataloging-in-Publication Data
Names: Engle, Margarita, author. | Palacios, Sara, illustrator.
Title: A song of frutas / Margarita Engle ; illustrated by Sara Palacios.
Description: First edition. | New York : Atheneum Books for Young Readers, [2021] | Audience: Ages 4–8. | Audience:
Grades 2–3. | Summary: While visiting her abuelo in Cuba, a young girl helps him sell frutas, singing the name of each
fruit as they walk, and after she returns to the United States, they exchange letters made of abrazos—hugs. Includes
historical and cultural notes.
Identifiers: LCCN 2020026214 | ISBN 9781534444898 (hardcover) | ISBN 9781534444904 (eBook)
Subjects: CYAC: Street vendors—Fiction. | Grandfathers—Fiction. | Fruit—Fiction. |
Cuban Americans—Fiction. | Cuba—Fiction.
Classification: LCC PZ7.E7158 Son 2021 | DDC [E]—dc23
LC record available at https://lccn.loc.gov/2020026214

For my nietos

—M. E.

For Mom and Dad, and for Ed

—S. P.

When we visit Abuelo, I help him sell frutas.
We sing the names of each fruit
as we walk, our footsteps like drumbeats,
our hands like maracas, shaking
bright food shapes
while we chant
with a rhythm:

toronja

naranja

piña

plátano

mango
limón
coco
melón   naranja
toronja
plátano
piña.

mango

coco

limón

melón

toro[n]

naranja

plátano

Our voices are bridges that reach up to windows,
inviting strangers to look out and become friends.
Smiling people perch on balconies,
listening to our cheerful music.

A few send baskets down
on ropes
to buy fruit
by placing
money inside,
and then waiting
until Abuelo sends
the basket
back up
filled with

mangos
lemons
limes
coconuts
melons
oranges
grapefruits
bananas
pineapples.

Whenever many lively pregoneros are all chanting
at the same time, Abuelo el frutero has to sing even louder,
his song as powerful as an opera star's glorious voice.

It's the only way to be heard
over the melodies and rhythms
of el tamalero who sells tamales
wrapped in slick green banana leaves,
and la yerbera with her fragrant herbs,

el viandero with sweet potatoes and yams,
and el manisero, the dancing vendor
    who offers cucuruchos—
pointy paper cones
        filled with mani,
    roasted peanuts
            that smell
            like
            the
                salty
                    blue
                    sea.

Best of all is la dulcera,
a woman with the voice
of an angel, who croons so sweetly
in praise of los caramelos—
chocolates and other delicious candies.
¡Sabroso!
Tasty!

My favorite visits to Abuelo
are on the eve of el año nuevo,
when everyone wants to buy
twelve grapes per person:
las uvas,
the fruit
of each new year's
good luck.

mango

limón

coco

melón

toronja

plátar

At midnight, I gobble
twelve grapes while I make
one wish per month for the whole
coming year.

My last wish is always
friendship between countries,
so that we can visit mi abuelo
more often, and maybe somehow,
someday,
he can also
fly high and wide
across the glittering
deep sea
to visit
us.

Each song I hear
on New Year's Eve
reminds me
that soon I'll return
to my own home.

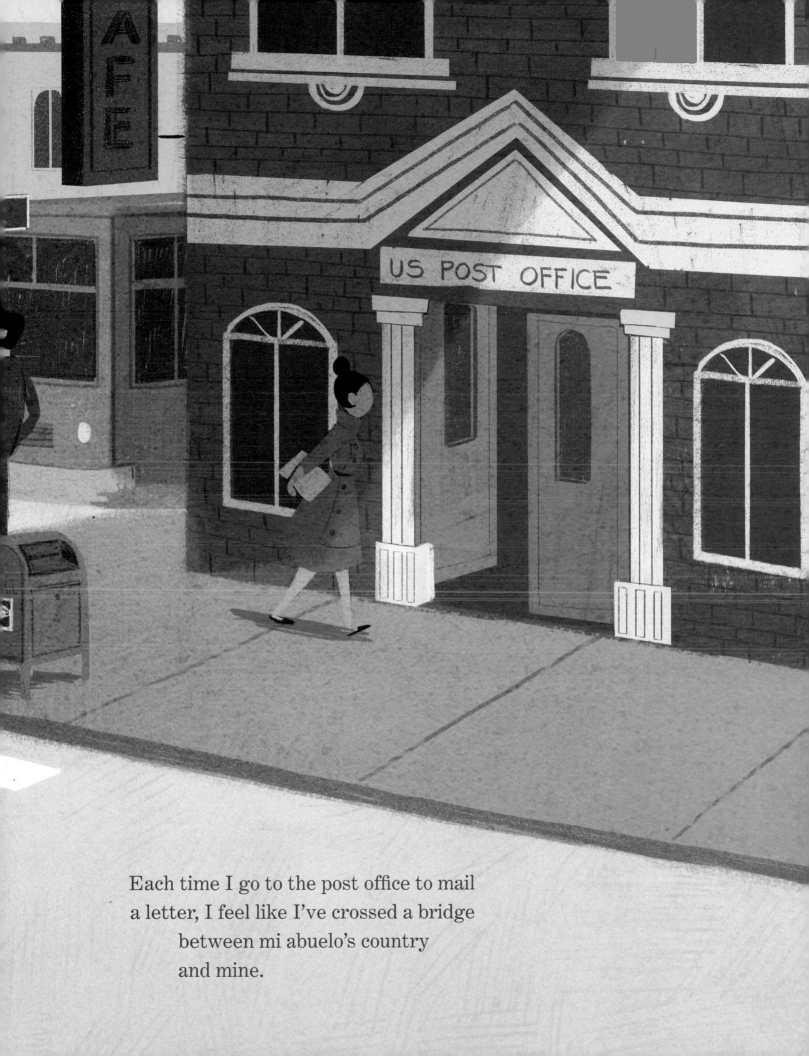

Each time I go to the post office to mail
a letter, I feel like I've crossed a bridge
between mi abuelo's country
and mine.

It would make me so sad
to live far apart from Abuelo
  if I didn't know that we can sing rhymes
  back and forth, verses on paper,
    all our hopeful poems flying like songbirds
    who glide and soar through wild sky,
      each syllable un abrazo,

a hug
made of
words.

AUTHOR'S NOTE

SPANGLISH

I wrote this poem in a mixture of English and Spanish because that is the way people talk on both shores of the strip of sea that separates Cuban and Cuban American family members.

TRAVEL RESTRICTIONS

Millions of Cuban American children in the United States do not have the chance to meet their overseas relatives due to travel restrictions imposed by authorities in both countries, who care more about politics than people. For more than half a century, countless Cuban American families have visited the island, either with or without permission, often in defiance of these travel restrictions— both as a pilgrimage of love for family members, and as an act of resistance against unfair rules. After an absence of thirty-one years, I began visiting relatives on the island in 1991, and I have continued visiting whenever I can.

LOS PREGONEROS

Los pregoneros are singing vendors who walk the streets of Cuba describing the things they sell in poetic ways, to attract customers. The historian Fernando Ortiz has described el pregón ("the vendor's song") as "el alma del cubano" ("the soul of a Cuban"). One of my great-uncles was a dairy farmer who delivered milk door-to-door in a jeep during the 1950s, but a few years earlier, los lecheros delivered milk by leading a cow from window to window, greeted by women holding empty bottles that were soon filled with fresh milk.

Celia Cruz sang about los fruteros and los dulceros, but the best-known song about a pregonero is "El Manisero," composed by Moisés Simons. "El Manisero" gained worldwide fame after it was recorded in New York in 1930, launching the international popularity of Cuban music and dance during the mid-twentieth century. The song grows louder, then fades away, to help the listener imagine a vendor's approach, followed by his departure as he moves on, still singing about peanuts in cucuruchos ("paper cones").

Los pregoneros and all other private businesses were outlawed in Cuba after the revolution. Selling things for profit was not permitted again until 2010. In the interim, vendors continued to operate quietly and secretly, in the "bolsa negra" ("black bag," or black market), whispering instead of singing.

NEW YEAR'S EVE

Grapes are rare in Cuba these days, but throughout Latin America, Spain, and Latino homes in the United States, many of us still follow the tradition of gobbling twelve grapes at midnight, while making one wish per month for the coming year.